W9-CFC-049

Early one morning the rising sun called,
"Wake up, wake up," and woke up the . . .

rooster.

"Cock-a-doodle-doo," said the rooster
and woke up the . . .

goose.

"Honk, honk," said the goose
and woke up the . . .

sheep.

"Baa, baa," said the sheep
and woke up the . . .

goat.

"Bleat, bleat," said the goat
and woke up the . . .

pig.

"Oink, oink," said the pig
and woke up the . . .

COW.

"Moo, moo," said the cow
and woke up the . . .

dog.

"Woof, woof," said the dog and woke up
the farmer. He climbed out of bed
and then went and fed . . .

the dog, the cow, the pig, the goat,
the sheep, the goose, and the rooster.